WALT DISNEY STUDIOS PRESENTS
A STUDIO GHIBLI FILM

MIYAZAKI'S
SPIRITED AWAY
Picture Book

Original Story and Screenplay Written and Directed by
Hayao Miyazaki

VIZ Media
San Francisco

Chihiro Ogino
An ordinary ten-year-old girl.

Chihiro's Mother and Father

Haku
The mysterious boy who helps Chihiro.

Yubaba
The witch who runs the Aburaya Bath House.

Baby
Yubaba's giant son.

Kamaji
An old man with six arms who runs the boiler room.

Yu-Bird
A bird with the face of Yubaba.

Kashira
Three heads that bounce around Yubaba's room.

Susuwatari
They help Kamaji carry coal. Their favorite food is confetti candy.

Lin
Chihiro's boss at the bath house. 14-years-old.

2

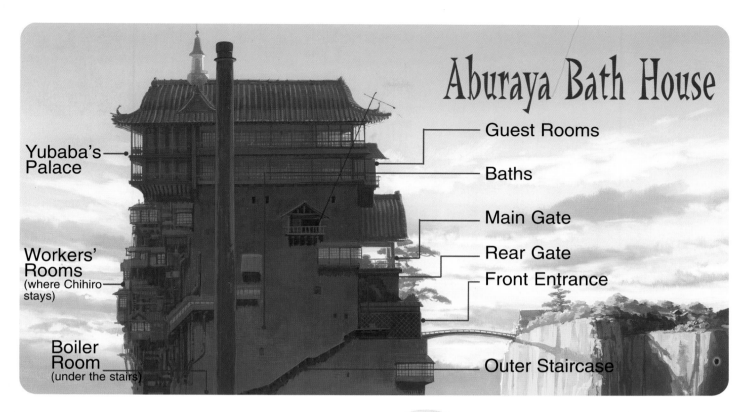

Aburaya Bath House

- Yubaba's Palace
- Workers' Rooms (where Chihiro stays)
- Boiler Room (under the stairs)
- Guest Rooms
- Baths
- Main Gate
- Rear Gate
- Front Entrance
- Outer Staircase

Assistant Manager
Manager
Frog men who are the boss of the workers at the bath house.

Little Green Frog
One of the workers.

Yuna
Slug women who take care of bath house guests.

No Face
A mysterious man from another world. He can only speak with the voices of people he swallows.

Zeniba
Yubaba's twin sister.

Bath House Guests

Stink Spirit

Daikon Radish Spirit

Ushioni

Onama

Kasuga

Otori

The Mysterious Country

"Chihiro? Chihiro? We're almost there!" Chihiro's father shouted from the driver's seat.

Today the Oginos were moving to their new house. Chihiro was sulking in the back seat of their car. She clutched her friend's going-away present, a bouquet of flowers.

"This really is in the middle of nowhere," her mother said.

Chihiro's father replied, "We'll just have to learn to like it. Look, Chihiro, there's your new school."

"It doesn't look so bad," her mother said. But Chihiro glanced gloomily out the window and muttered, "It's gonna stink. I liked my old school."

The car climbed up the hill towards the houses.

Everything about the move, including the new town and the new school, bothered Chihiro.

They drove down a narrow road leading into a forest. Father had taken a wrong turn.

Father refused to turn back.

"This road should get us there," he insisted and drove into the forest.

The forest grew
thick and dark.

They passed a
statue covered with
moss that
scared
Chihiro.

WE'RE FINE.

"It looks like an entrance."
Her father slammed on the
brakes in front of a red gate.

But the gate was too small for
the car.

FWEEEE!

The wind whistled beyond the tunnel.

Leaves rustled at Chihiro's feet

and drifted into the tunnel.

"The wind's pulling us in…" Chihiro looked into the tunnel, terrified.

Father said, "Come on, let's go in. I want to see what's on the other side."

"I'm not going. It gives me the creeps, Dad."

"Don't be such a scaredy-cat, Chihiro. Let's just take a look."

"I'm not going."

But Father and Mother kept going into the tunnel. Left alone, Chihiro chased after them.

"Wait for me!"

She could only hear their footsteps echoing in the tunnel.

They came out onto a strange wide-open field.

A red clock tower loomed under the blue sky. There was an abandoned house and old statues…

"Now let's go back," Chihiro begged her parents, but they kept going forward.

They crossed the
field and reached a
dry river bed.
Suddenly, a
delicious odor
drifted by them.

Her parents climbed the
stone stairs and followed
the smell.

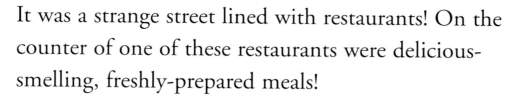

It was a strange street lined with restaurants! On the counter of one of these restaurants were delicious-smelling, freshly-prepared meals!

"Hello, in there! Does anybody work here?" Father shouted, but there was no answer.

Mother then said, "Don't worry, honey. We can pay the bill when they get back."

"Good idea."

Chihiro's parents sat down and began eating the food on the counter.

"Let's just get out of here!" Chihiro said, but her parents were too preoccupied with eating.

Chihiro gave up and left the restaurant. She looked around. The street was quiet. In the distance there was a red lantern at the top of the stone stairs.

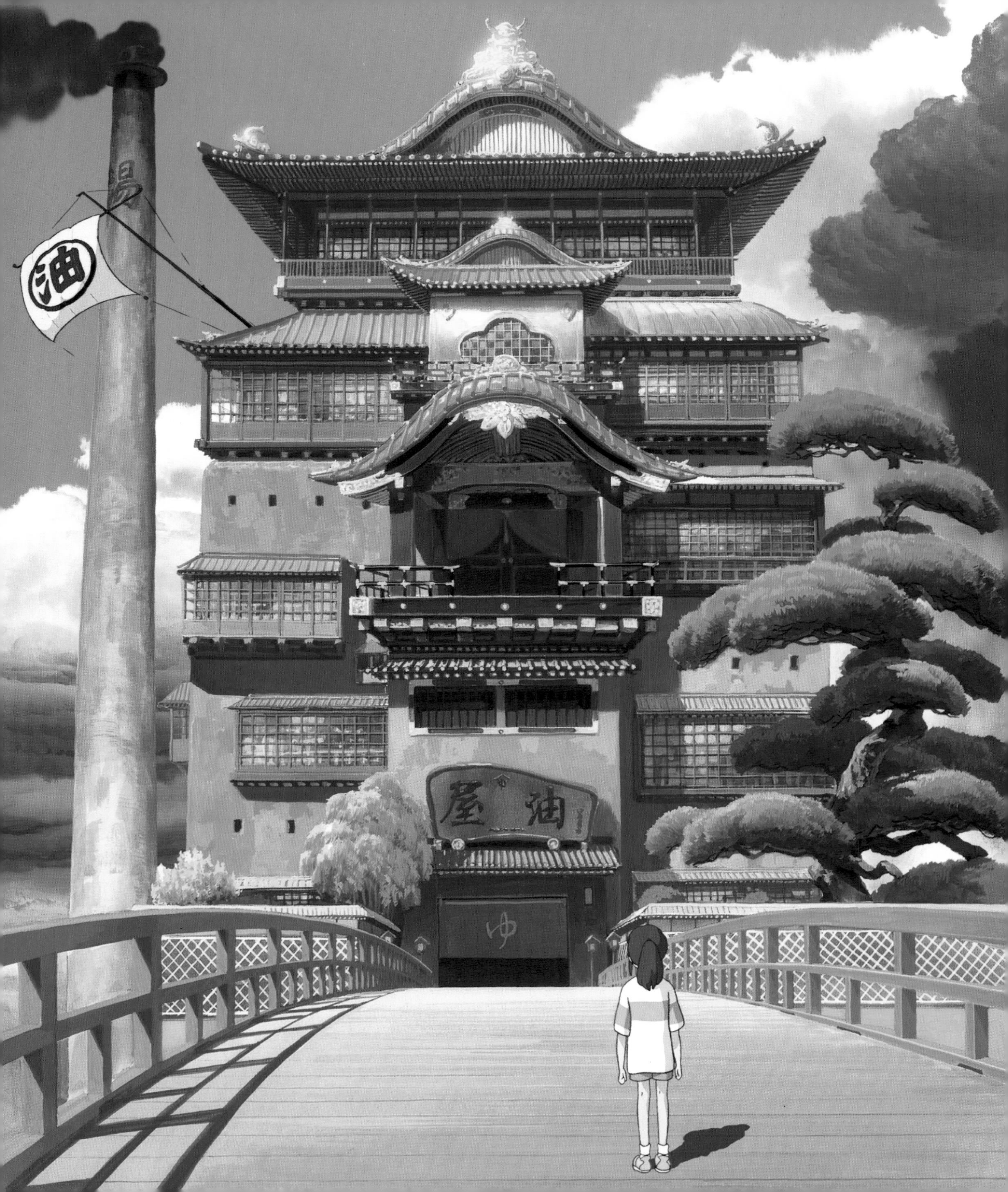

油
油屋
ゆ

She climbed the stairs and stood still when she reached the top. A giant building towered over the crimson-red bridge.

Chihiro looked up at the gaudy building in the afternoon sun.

"That's weird…"

It had a sign that read, "ABURAYA." It had a tall chimney too. Could it be a bath house then?

RRRRR. She heard a train roaring under the bridge.

She leaned over the rail. There wasn't any water underneath, just a railroad. The train ran along the bottom of a dark valley.

That was when Chihiro noticed a boy standing next to her.

He was staring at her. Then as he suddenly realized something, he glared at her and said, "You shouldn't be here. Get out of here. Now!"

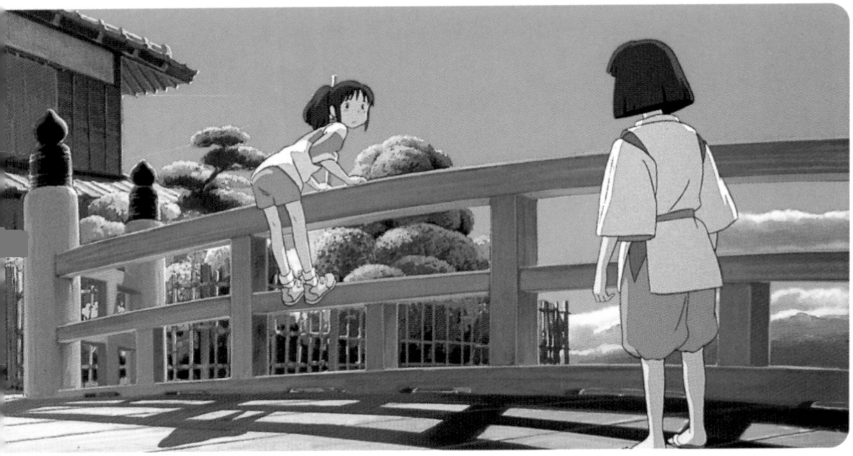

"What?"
"It's almost night. Leave before it gets dark."

It was getting dark all of a sudden and the

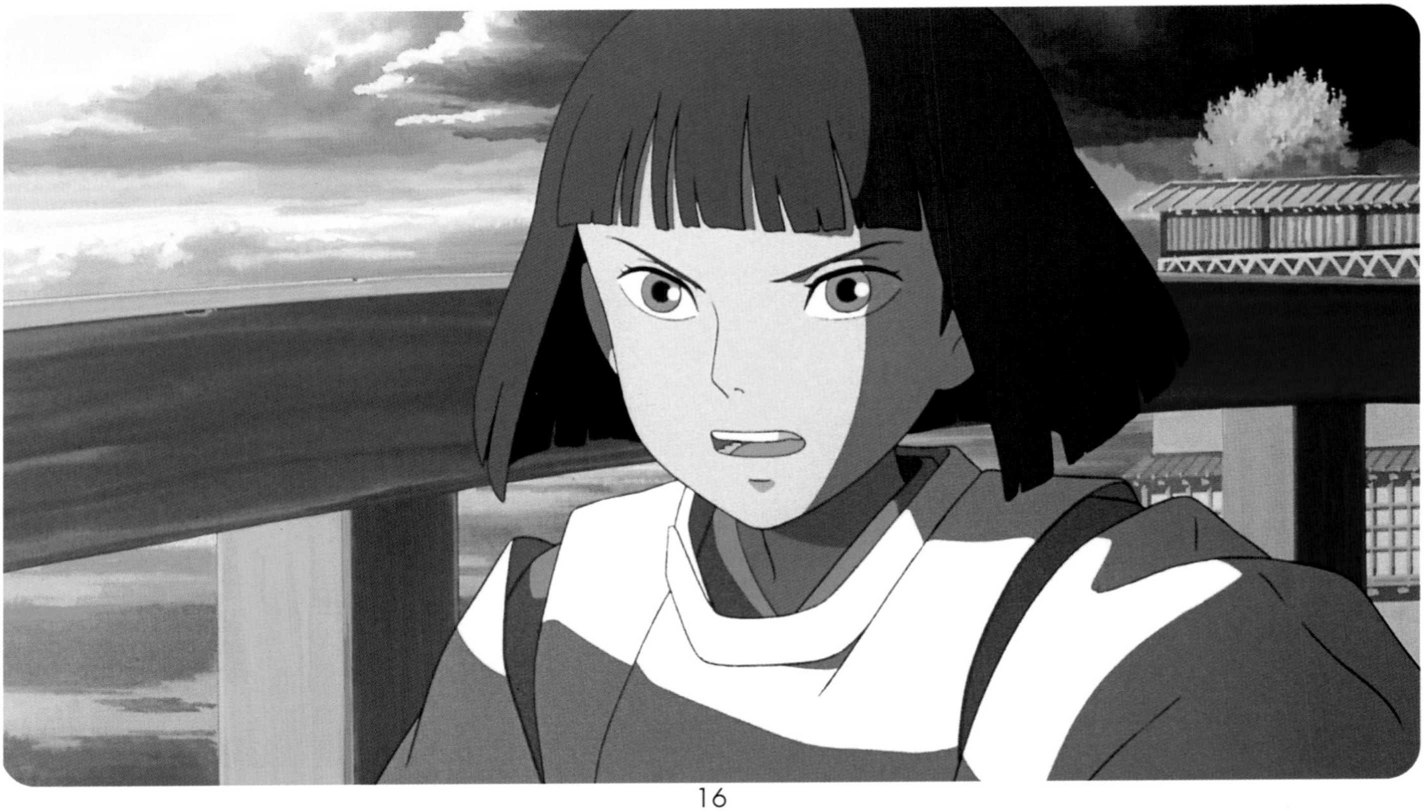

building's lamps began to glow.

"They're lighting the lamps. Get out of here! You've got to get across the river. Go!" Confused, Chihiro started to run.

By the time she reached the stairs, though, it was dark.

Chihiro was frightened. She ran into the restaurant to find her parents.

"Mom! Dad! Let's get out of here!" She grabbed her father, who slowy turned around.

They weren't her parents!

They were two pigs!
"Ahhhhh!" Chihiro ran
down the street.

Dark shadows drifted by.

"Daaaad! Moooom!"
Chihiro hurried back the
way they'd come.

But look what she found!

The field they had crossed had turned into a river.

She saw the clock tower far away on the other side of the wide river.

A glowing ferry floated on the dark water and approached the shore.

"I'm dreaming. Come on, wake up! Wake up!"

WHAT? I'M DREAMING! I'M DREAMING!

She kneeled down and buried her face in her hands. She looked at her hands and screamed, "I'm see-thru! It's just a bad dream!"

Then she could hear loud music. The passengers of the ferry had arrived...

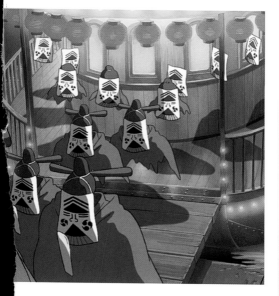

"Ahhhhh!" Chihiro screamed and ran away.

She hid in a dark spot when someone suddenly came up from behind.

It was the boy she had met on the bridge!

"Don't be afraid. I just want to help." The boy gently spoke to

the terrified girl, offering her a small tablet. "Open your mouth and eat this. You have to eat some food from this world or else you'll disappear."

"Don't worry, it won't turn you into a pig. Chew it and swallow."
The boy pressed the tablet to her mouth.

Chihiro swallowed the tablet. The boy took her by the hand and
said, "There you go. You're all better. Now, come with me."

"Where's my mom and dad?
They…didn't really turn
into pigs, did they?"

"You can't see them now, but
you will."

"Don't move!" The boy shielded Chihiro while he looked up at the sky.

There was a scary-looking bird flying in the sky. It had a human head. The human-headed bird's eyes gleamed, as if it were searching for something. Then it flew away.

"That bird's looking for you. You've got to get out of here."

The boy placed his hand over Chihiro's leg and quietly chanted, "In the name of the wind and water within thee, unbind her."

Then he took her by the hand and started to run.

Was he using magic? Chihiro couldn't believe how fast they were running through the alleys!

They arrived at the bridge
she saw earlier that day.
What was this place?

The building glowed
mysteriously. A crowd of the
strange beings she saw on the
ferry crossed the bridge.

"Welcome."

"Always nice to see you."

They were being greeted by
frog men.

The boy said…

"You have to hold your breath while we cross the bridge. Even the tiniest breath will break the spell, and then everyone will see you."

The boy addressed one of the frog men, "I'm back from my mission."

"Welcome back, Master Haku."

It seemed like the frog men couldn't see Chihiro!

Chihiro held her breath and held on tight to the boy as they crossed the bridge.

They sneaked into the garden.

"You can't stay here, they'll find you. I'll create a diversion while you escape…"

"No, don't leave me. I don't want to be alone."

Chihiro begged him to stay.

"You have no choice, if you want to help your parents…This is what you have to do."

"They did turn into pigs! I wasn't dreaming."

The boy touched her forehead and whispered, "Now, when things quiet down, go out through the back gate."

And with these words, images appeared in her head.

Go all the way down the stairs…

…until you reach the boiler room.

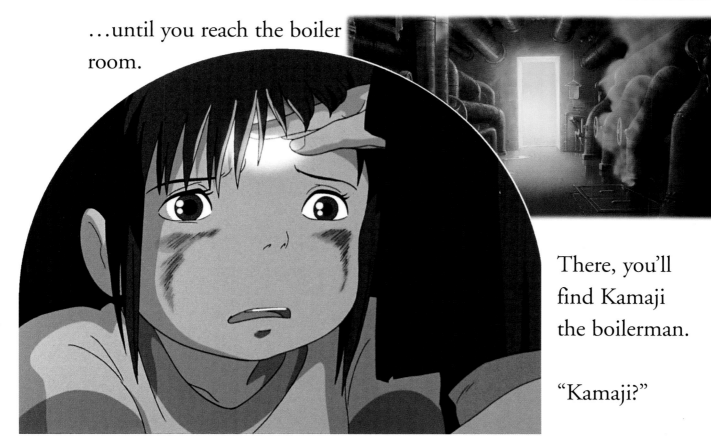

There, you'll find Kamaji the boilerman.

"Kamaji?"

"Tell him you want to work here, even if he refuses, you must insist. If you don't get a job, Yubaba will turn you into an animal."

"Yubaba? Huh?"

"You'll see. She's the witch who rules the bath house. Kamaji will try to turn you away or trick you into leaving but just keep asking for work. It'll be hard work, but you'll be able to stay here. Then even Yubaba can't harm you."

Chihiro nodded and the boy said, "And don't forget, Chihiro. I'm your friend."

"How did you know my name's Chihiro?"

"I've known you since you were very small. My name is Haku." Then he left her and entered the building.

> **AUGH!**

Yubaba's Contract

Just as Haku had told her, there were stairs beyond the rear gate.

The train ran down far below.

The stairs in the dark had no railing. Chihiro carefully went down them.

Finally she reached the bottom of the stairs and slowly opened the door to the boiler room.

An old man sat in front of the roaring red-hot boiler. Could he be Kamaji?

Below him, little Susuwatari busily carried coal while the old man skillfully used all six of his arms.

So Kamaji wasn't human? Chihiro was shocked.

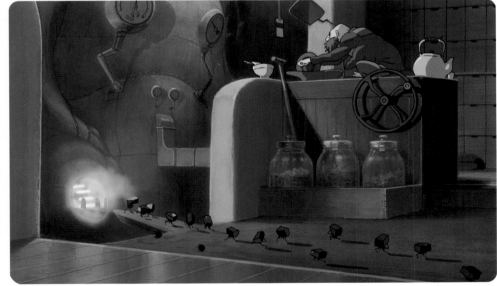

Chihiro followed Haku's instructions. She raised her voice and asked, "Uh, hello, are you Kamaji? Haku told me to come here and ask you for work. Could you give me a job, please?"

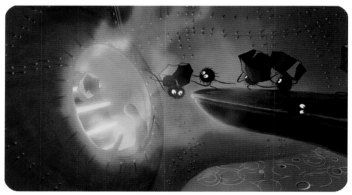

"Eh?' The old man turned around, looked over Chihiro, and replied, "Yeah, I'm Kamaji, slave to the boiler that heats the baths!"

"I don't need any help. The place is full of soot. I just cast a spell on them and I've got all the workers I need."

Kamaji and the Susuwatari continued with their work as if they couldn't be bothered by someone like Chihiro.

Tokens tied to ropes fell from a hole in the ceiling.

After he read each token, Kamaji took various herbs out of the drawers behind him and crushed them together with his flexible arms.

"TWEE TWEE." A small Susuwatari was squashed by a big piece of coal.

Chihiro went to help him, but the coal wouldn't budge. It was much heavier than it looked.

She finally managed to lift it up. The small Susuwatari scuttled away into a hole.

"What should I do with this?"

"Uh, should I leave it here?"

She was about to put it down when Kamaji yelled at her, "Finish what you started, human!"

All right then! Chihiro was determined now. Tottering along with the Susuwatari, she carried her piece of coal and tossed it into the red-hot boiler.

"Chow time!"

A girl with a wooden tub arrived to deliver their meals. She was shocked at the sight of Chihiro.

"A human! You're in trouble! You're the one everyone's looking for!"

But Kamaji said, "She's my granddaughter. She says she wants to work here, but I've got all the help I need. Will you take her to see Yubaba?"

Then he said to Chihiro, ""If you want a job, you'll have to make a deal with Yubaba. She's the head honcho here."

Lin then replied gruffly,
"Come on, little girl."

Chihiro stepped onto the floor
and Lin glared back at her.
"Can't you even manage a 'Yes
ma'am' or a 'Thank you'?"

"Ye-Yes ma'am."

"What a dope. Hurry up."

"Yes ma'am."

"Thank the boilerman, you
idiot, you know he's really
sticking his neck out for you."

Chihiro bowed to Kamaji.

"Thank you, Mr. Boilerman."

GOOD
LUCK.

parlor rooms were crowded with guests.

Chihiro busily looked around as she followed Lin.

HURRY UP.

"We have to go all the way to the top floor. That's where Yubaba lives."

Lin tried not to exchange looks with anyone as they took the elevators to the top of the building.

The top floors looked like a fancy hotel. The halls and

There was a bridge over the large atrium.

The baths were under the bridge.

Chihiro saw strange guests relaxing in their baths under the steam.

There was one more elevator to the top floor. Suddenly a frog man called out, "Lin, what's that smell?"

Lin quickly nudged Chihiro into the elevator.

Chihiro was left alone with a giant radish-shaped guest inside the elevator. She had no idea what to do.

The top floor was dim, but gold was shining everywhere.

YOU SMELL JUST LIKE A HUMAN.

OH, REALLY?

The guest looked around, but decided not to go out. He bowed to Chihiro and returned to the elevator.

Chihiro nervously bowed back to him.

She stood in front of a large door, alone.

What was going to happen to her? Summoning all her courage, she tried to open the door.

YOU'RE THE MOST PATHETIC LITTLE GIRL I'VE EVER SEEN.

"Aren't you even going to knock?" the door knocker croaked. Its eyes were wide open.

Chihiro tucked in her hands and the door swung open.

"Well, come in."

A strange force sucked Chihiro in.

Each door proceeded to open and then shut as Chihiro was sucked in further and further until she reached a room with a fireplace.

"Oy Oy Oy." Three strange-looking heads bounced around Chihiro.

"Quiet down, you're making a racket."

Chihiro looked over and saw a large-headed old woman sitting behind her desk on the other side of the room.

It was Yubaba!

"I was wondering if you could give me a job!" Chihiro said.

Yubaba slowly lifted her face up and said, "I don't want to hear such a stupid request. And this is certainly no place for humans. It's a bath house for the spirits. It's where they come to rest and replenish themselves.

"And you humans always make a mess of things. Like your parents who gobbled up the food of the spirits like pigs! They got what they deserved. And you should be punished, too."

"Please, can't you give me a job?"

"Don't start that again!"

"Please, I just want to work!"

"Don't say that!"

Yubaba flew at her in a rage.

"You're a spoiled kid, so there's no job for you. Now get out! Or maybe I'll give you the most difficult job I've got, and work you until you breathe your very last breath."

Yubaba dug her nails into Chihiro's neck.

BOOM! KRAK! Something
shattered. A giant foot burst
through the other side of the
door behind the curtain.

"Waa! Waa!" It was the sound
of a baby crying.

Yubaba ran to the
door and purred. It
was as if she
suddenly became a
different person,
"Mommy's here.
What's wrong?"

Chihiro had no idea what
was happening, but she
kept asking, "I want you
to give me a job, please!"

"Quiet down, you're scaring the baby."
Yubaba was in a panic.

"I'm not leaving until you give me a job!"

"Okay, okay, just be quiet!"

A sheet of paper and a pen floated towards Chihiro.

"That's your contract. Sign your name away. And I'll put you to work. If I hear even one little complaint out of you, you'll be joining your parents in the pig pen."

"I can't believe I took that oath to give a job to anyone who asks," Yubaba muttered.

After Chihiro signed her name, the contract glided back into Yubaba hand.

"So your name's Chihiro? What a pretty name."

Yubaba then placed her hand over her name...

The characters of her name floated upward.

Yubaba wrapped her fingers around them.

"From now on,

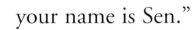

your name is Sen."

"You got that? Answer me, Sen!"

"Ye-Yes, ma'am."

Yubaba called for Haku. "This girl signed a contract. Set her up with a job."

Haku gave Chihiro a cold look and asked, "What's your name?"

"What?" Taken aback by Haku, who suddenly seemed so cold, Chihiro answered, "Oh, it's Sen."

"Okay, Sen. Follow me."

Haku introduced Chihiro to the other workers and assigned her to work with Lin.

Once they were alone, Lin smiled enthusiastically and exclaimed,

"I can't believe you pulled it off! You're such a dope, I was really worried. Now, keep on your toes. And if you need anything, ask me."

Lin took Chihiro to their room.

"Lin, there aren't two people called Haku here, are there?"

"Two Hakus? I can barely stand one. He's Yubaba's henchman, don't trust anything he says."

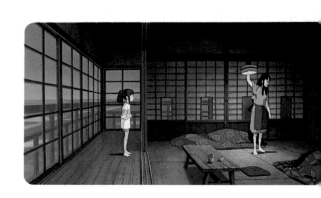

Morning came. Their work done, the workers went to bed.

Someone sneaked into the quiet room and gently woke up Chihiro.

"Meet me at the bridge. I'll take you to your parents."

She woke up and looked around. There was no one in sight.

But Chihiro knew it was Haku.

She rushed to the bridge, where a black shadow wearing a mask stood in the morning light, staring at her.

Was was he a guest?

Chihiro bowed to him as she walked past him.

After crossing the bridge she looked back, but the man had vanished.

Then Haku appeared.

FOLLOW ME.

Haku took Chihiro to the pig pen. There were pigs everywhere. Chihiro ran over to two pigs that Haku pointed out to her.

"Mom, Dad! It's me… Se-Sen."

But they did not respond to her.

"They ate too much. They're sleeping it off. They don't remember being human."

"Don't you worry, I promise I'll get you out of here soon. Just don't get any fatter, or they'll eat you!" Chihiro burst out of the pig pen.

Outside, Chihiro crouched down. Haku returned her clothes. "Hide them. You'll need them to get home."

She found something in her clothes.

"My goodbye card's still here...."

Chihiro stared at the card.

"Chi-hi-ro...That's my name, isn't it!"

She couldn't believe she had forgotten her name.

home. I've tried everything to remember mine."

"That's how Yubaba controls you, by stealing your name. So hold on to that card. Keep it hidden. And while you're here, you must call yourself Sen."

"I can't believe I forgot my name. She almost took it from me."

"If you completely forget it, you'll never find your way

"You can't remember your name?"

BUT FOR SOME REASON, I REMEMBER YOUR NAME.

"I put a spell on it, so it'll give you back your strength. Just eat it."

"Here you go. Eat this. You must be hungry." Haku offered her a rice ball.

Chihiro forced herself to take a bite.

"No."

One bite was enough to

restore her appetite. She ate the rice balls quickly. Her sadness returned with her appetite, and she burst into tears.

Tears streamed down Chihiro's cheeks. She couldn't stop crying.

Haku gently urged Chihiro, "Have some more. You'll be all right."

Chihiro continued to cry as she ate the rice balls.

Haku saw her off at the foot of the bridge.

"Just stay out of trouble."

"Thank you, Haku. You're a good friend."

Chihiro returned to the bath house, feeling much better.

She crossed the bridge and turned around. She saw something white climbing the sky.

It looked like a dragon.

The white dragon,
shining in the
morning light, faded
into the blue sky.

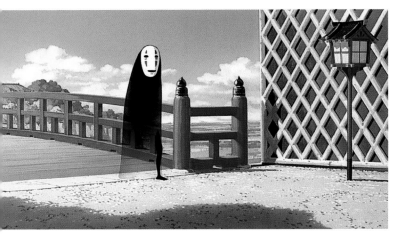

The Bath House Guest

As the sun went down another day at the bath house began. The workers hustled to prepare the bath house for business.

Under Lin's supervision, Chihiro worked hard at her new job. As she emptied her bucket of water in the garden, she saw someone standing there. It was the masked man she saw earlier, now standing quietly alone in the rain.

GEEZ, SEN. HAVEN'T YOU EVER WORKED A DAY IN YOUR LIFE?

"Hello? Aren't you getting wet out there?" Chihiro asked,
but the man remained silent.

"I'll leave the door open for you."

Chihiro left the glass door open and returned to work.

The masked man cautiously
entered the deserted hall.

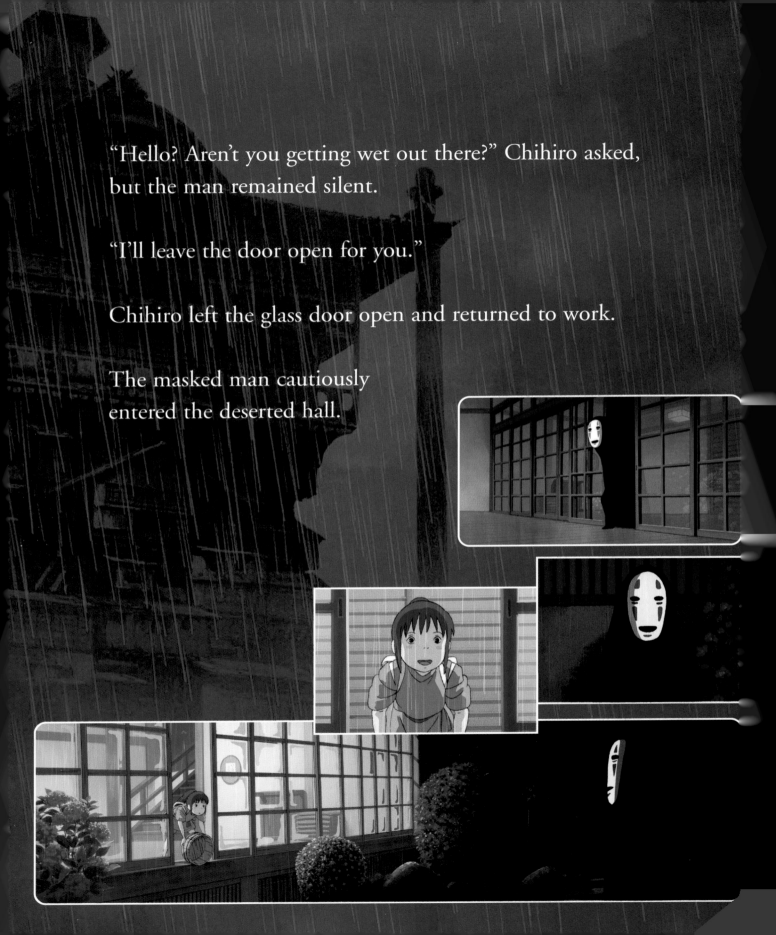

Lin and Chihiro were assigned to take care of the big tub for a guest.

The big tub was incredibly filthy.

THEY HAVEN'T CLEANED THIS TUB IN MONTHS.

Lin and Chihiro got to work cleaning the tub. But no matter how hard they tried wiping it, the sludge caked on the tub would not come off.

"We only use this tub for our really filthy guests," Lin explained. "We'll have to soak it off. Get an herbal soak from the foreman."

"A what?"

"An herbal soak token."

The foreman refused to give Chihiro any tokens.

"I can't waste a token on you. Scrub it yourself. I said scrub it yourself."

Chihiro was in trouble. Then the masked man suddenly appeared out of nowhere. He bowed to Chihiro.

Chihiro bowed back as the man vanished.

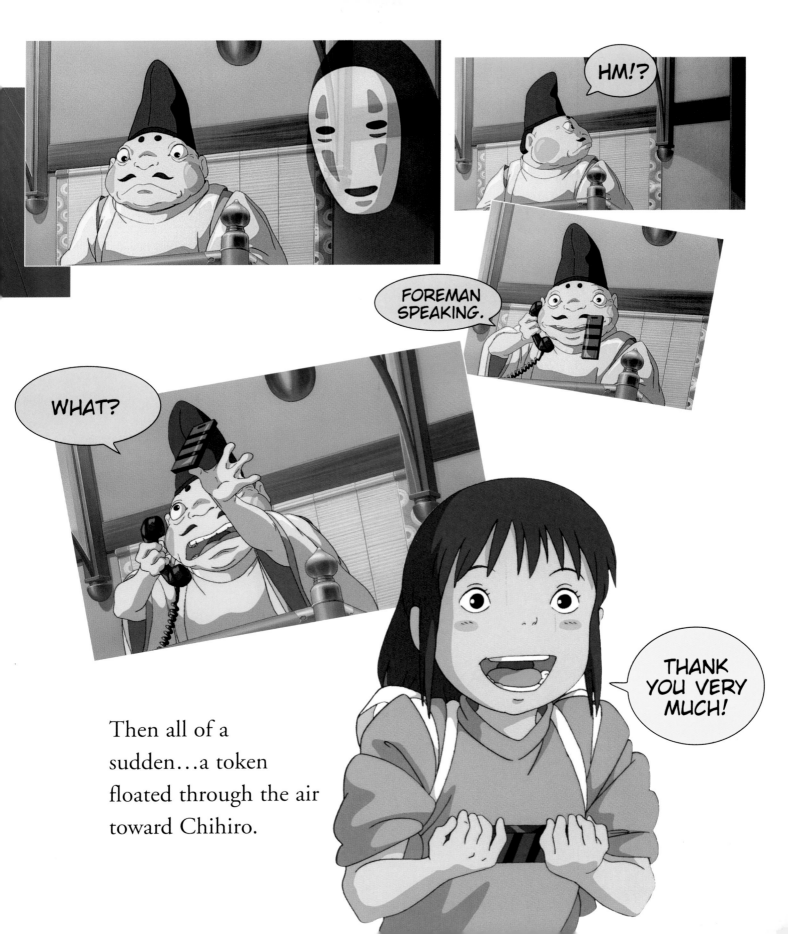

Then all of a sudden...a token floated through the air toward Chihiro.

Lin looked at the token Chihiro gave her and said, "Wow, Sen, you got a really good one."

Lin clipped the token onto a rope hanging from a hole in the wall. Kamaji prepared the herbal soak assigned on the token.

The masked man appeared again. He had a
handful of tokens.

"Ah…ah…"

He offered them to Chihiro.

"Thanks, but I don't need anymore.
No, I only need one," Chihiro
replied. The man vanished, leaving
behind the tokens.

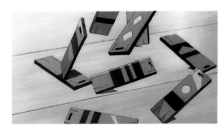

Meanwhile, trouble was brewing in the baths. A frightening guest was coming.

Yubaba called Chihiro and told her, "Sen, don't mess this up. Take this guest to the big tub and take care of him. You hear me!?"

72

A Stink Spirit arrived covered in sludge.

His stench was dizzying.

HUH!?

"Don't make him wait, Sen! Get him to the bath!" Yubaba yelled at her.

Chihiro showed the Stink Spirit to the big tub.

The big tub became a sea of sludge.

The Stink Spirit was still as dirty as ever, even after plunging into the bath. He looked over at Chihiro and moaned, as if he were trying to tell her something.

"URR—"

"What? Just a minute, sir."

That's right, she thought, I'll request another herbal soak from Kamaji! Chihiro took one of her extra tokens and clipped it on to the rope from the wall.

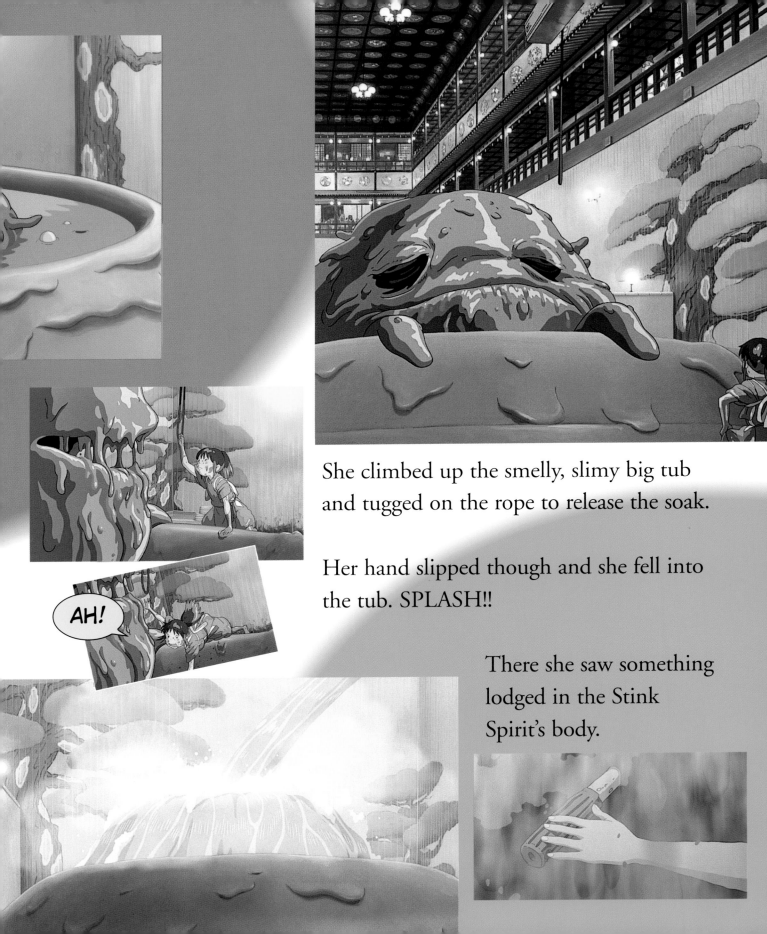

She climbed up the smelly, slimy big tub
and tugged on the rope to release the soak.

Her hand slipped though and she fell into
the tub. SPLASH!!

There she saw something
lodged in the Stink
Spirit's body.

AH!

Lin came to her rescue.

"Sen, are you all right?"

"Lin! I think he needs help. It feels like there's a thorn in his side."

"A thorn?"

"It won't come out."

Yubaba exclaimed, "Listen to me. That's no Stink Spirit we have on

EVERYONE READY ON MY COMMAND! AND HEAVE!

YOU'RE GOING TO BE FINE. I WON'T LET HIM HURT YOU.

our hands." She produced a rope out of thin air.

"Grab on to this rope!" With the rope tied to the thorn, everyone began tugging as hard as they could.

All together now, heave! And heave!

SHLIP! SHLIP! An old bicycle first popped out, and then…

FWOOOSH! A ton of garbage came bursting out with the sludge.

The water rushed around Chihiro.

HEAVE!

Immersed underwater,
Chihiro saw something
strange.

A giant old man's mask came floating up from the still
water into the steam. "Well done." The dignified voice
echoed majestically.

The water washed away and Chihiro's body was completely

cleansed. In her hand she found a dumpling.

The sludge on the floor became clear now and something shined underneath.

"Gold nuggets! It's gold!"

Everyone cried for joy.

SPLASH!
The old
man's mask
came
bursting
out of the
tub. His dragon's body
flew up to the ceiling.

"HA HA HA HA…"
His wonderful laugh
echoed through the
bath house.

"Open the gates. Make way for our guest!" Yubaba shouted and the spirits opened the gate.

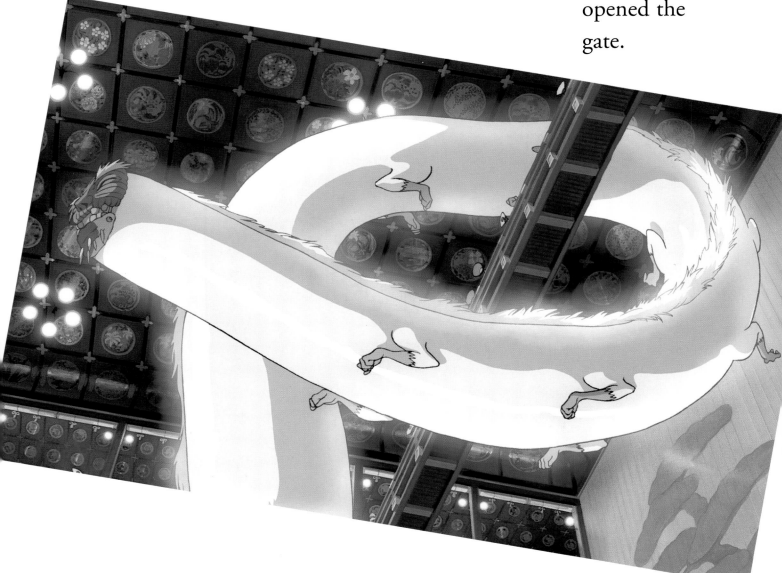

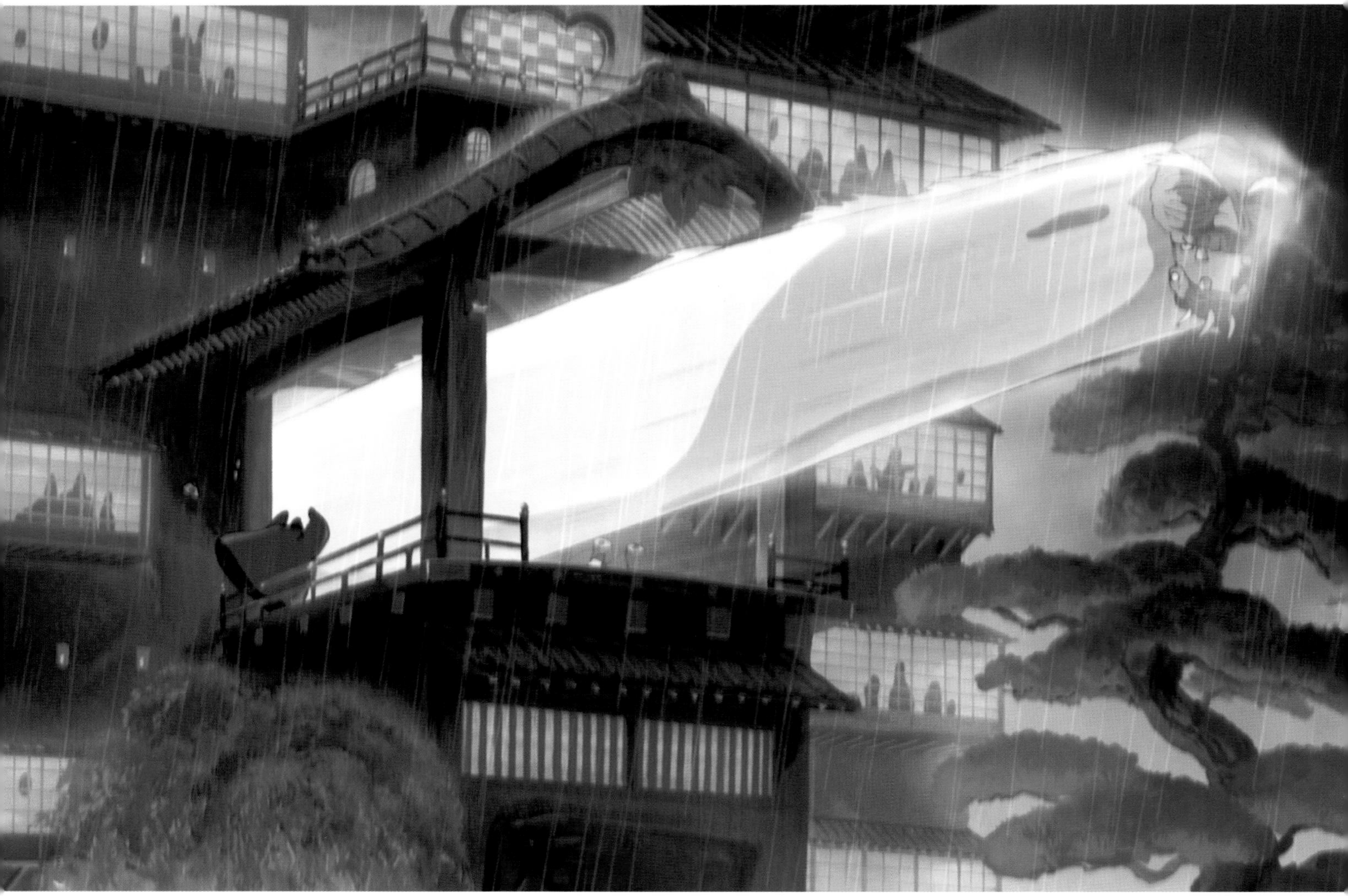

FWOOSH! The dragon flew out of the gate like the wind, vanishing into the rainy evening sky.

"Hurray! Hurray!" The spirits were also shouting for joy.

Yubaba hugged Chihiro and said, "Sen, you did great! We made so much money!"

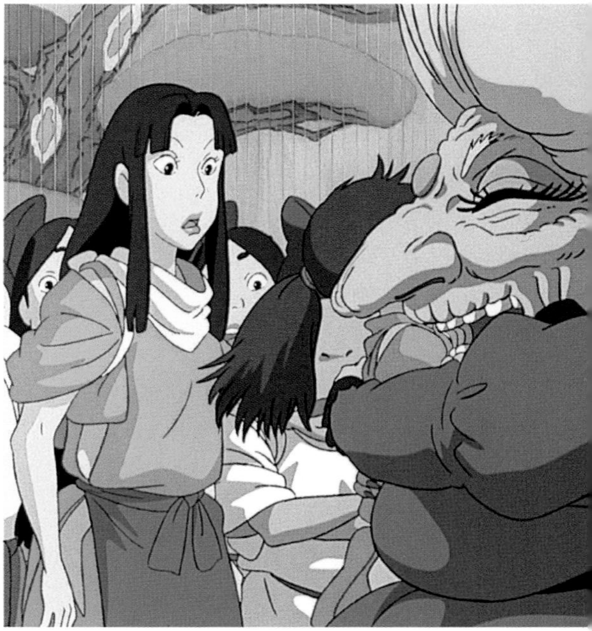

"That spirit is rich and powerful. Everyone, learn from Sen."

Chihiro was so happy. She gently pressed the dumpling in her hands against her chest.

Meanwhile, behind the crowd in the corner, the masked man was staring at his hand.

And so Chihiro's first day of work came to an end.

Chihiro took a bite from the sweet bun Lin gave her and said, "Haku wasn't there."

"He just disappears sometimes. Rumor has it that he runs around doing Yubaba's dirty work."

"Really…"

Because of the rain, the entire area below had turned into an ocean. A train slid over the water.

THANK YOU.

HERE.

Chihiro wrapped her fingers around the dumpling the river spirit gave her. She thought it might turn her mother and father back into human beings. She smiled and took a small bite of the dumpling.

But it was so bitter she had to get the taste out of her mouth by taking another bite from her sweet bun.

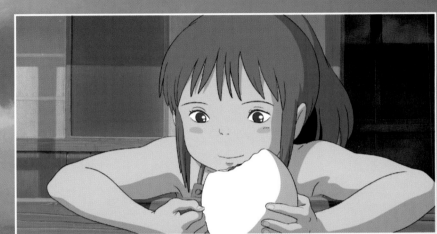

UNGH!?

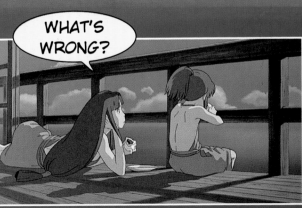

WHAT'S WRONG?

After everyone had gone to bed, the little green frog quietly sneaked up to the big tub. He was looking for more gold nuggets.

Suddenly, the masked man appeared from the tub and offered his hand.

"Ah…ah…"

Gold nuggets came spilling out of his hands.

"You can make gold?" The little green frog approached him.

GIMME!

And the masked man quickly
swallowed the little green
frog up.

"What's going on in there?"
The assistant manager
showed up.

"Hey boss, I'm hungry!"

"I know that voice!" Looking
up, he saw the masked man
squatting there like a frog.

The masked man sprinkled
gold nuggets and spoke in
the little green frog's voice,
"Here, I'll pay you up front.
And I want to take a bath,
too. Why don't you wake
everyone up!"

Chihiro woke up that afternoon. The room was deserted. The sun was still up, so it wasn't time for work yet. What was going on? Chihiro wondered. She went into the hall.

Lin came up to her and said, "Look, it's real gold. There's a new guest here who's loaded. He's giving gold away by the handfuls."

There was a masked man who was eating up all the meals they offered and who was tossing gold at them!

"Come on," Lin said and ran out for more gold.

Chihiro didn't care about gold. She returned to her room and stared out the window.

She saw the pig pen where her parents were. She wondered how they were doing.

Suddenly, a white dragon burst out from the water, climbing up the sky. It was the dragon she saw yesterday by the bridge!

The dragon was being chased by what looked like a flock of white birds.

"Haku, fight them! Come on,

this way!" She yelled impulsively, then wondered how she knew the dragon was Haku.

Perhaps Chihiro's voice had reached her, for the dragon came crashing into her room. Chihiro quickly began closing the glass doors.

The white objects fluttered onto the floor. What she thought were birds were only paper dolls.

Chihiro said to the wounded

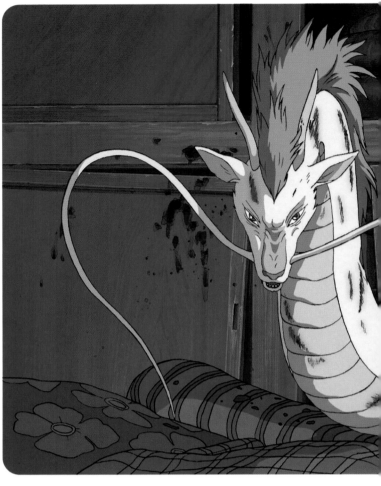

dragon, "Haku? You're bleeding."

"HAHH, HAHH."

The dragon had the

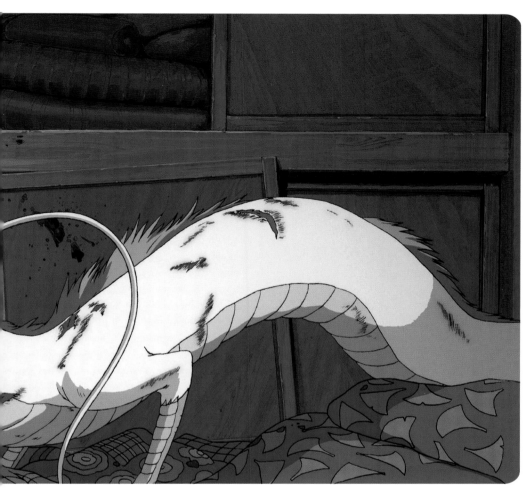

ing, it stared back at Chihiro.

"Hold still. Those paper things are gone now. You're going to be all right."

same eyes as Haku's, but now they were gleaming like the eyes of a beast. Huffing and puff-

"HAHH—!"

The dragon leaped outside, leaving behind a trail of blood.

Chihiro ran and leaned over the railing covered with blood. She looked for the dragon. It struggled up towards the top of the building.

"He went in that top window. I've got to get there before he bleeds to death!" Chihiro ran out of the room.

One of the dolls suddenly stood up and clung to Chihiro's back. Chihiro was so focused on climbing the stairs she didn't notice it.

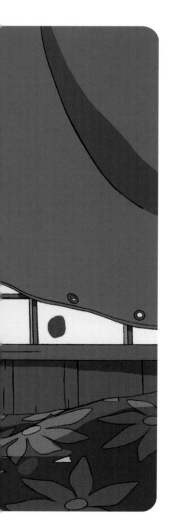

Upstairs, the bath house was in an uproar. Everyone surrounded the masked man, flattering him for more gold nuggets.

"Thank you for helping me earlier." Chihiro thanked him for the herbal soak tokens he had given her. Then the masked man offered his hands to her.

"Ah…ah…"

A mound of gold nuggets came rising out of his hands.

Chihiro shook her head and flatly refused, "I don't want any."

"Eh? Eh?" The masked man was confused, because she didn't want any of the gold everyone else wanted so badly.

"I'm sorry, but I'm in a really big hurry." Chihiro bowed quickly and ran off.

The assistant manager offered an apology, "I am terribly sorry, Sir. You'll have to excuse the little girl. She's just a human…"

The masked man looked down and yelled at him, "Wipe that smile off your face."

He grabbed both the assistant manager and a woman nearby and

swallowed them both.

"Ahhh! He ate them!"

"Aieeee!"

Everyone fled in fear. Now the bath house was in chaos!

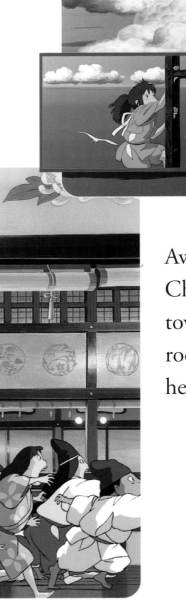

Away from this, Chihiro hurried towards Yubaba's room. All she had on her mind was Haku.

The Witch's Seal

Chihiro sneaked through the window into Yubaba's palace. It looked like a baby's room. There were pillows and toys all over the floor. But everything was so huge, it was like a giant's room too.

Suddenly she heard Yubaba's voice.

"We're in a big mess. I found out who our rich customer is. He's a No Face. It's all your fault. You're so greedy. You attract terrible guests."

Chihiro peeked in and found Yubaba on the phone.

"Don't let him eat anyone else 'til I get down there."

Yubaba hung up the phone and ordered the Kashira, "Get him out of here. He'll be dead soon anyway."

Was this about Haku? Chihiro looked in when she saw Yubaba coming. Chihiro leaped into the mound of pillows.

Yubaba came near the mound of pillows and examined it. There was a giant baby under them!

"Awww!"

Yubaba pampered the baby, who frowned in his sleep.

"I'm sorry. Let me give you a kiss. Go back to sleep now," she said and left the room.

Relieved, Chihiro was about to leave the room—but she was yanked back by the baby!

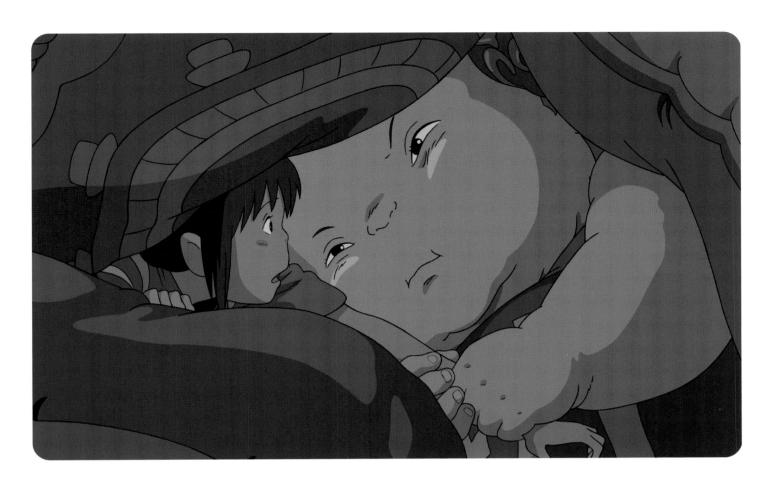

"Play with me."

"Listen, someone very important to me is terribly hurt. I've got to go right now, so please let go of me."

"If you go, I'll cry. And Mama will hear me, and Mama will come in here and kill you."

"Germs! I've got germs, see?" Chihiro stuck her bloody arm in front of Baby's eyes. Baby was terrified by this and screamed, "Waaaah!" and let go of Chihiro.

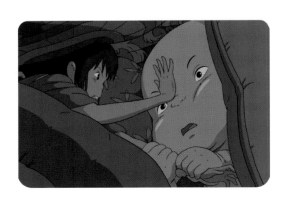

Chihiro ran into the next room and saw the Kashira dragging the dragon towards the hole in the middle of the room.

"Haku! Are you okay?"

The Yu-Bird shrieked and attacked Chihiro as she held onto the dragon.

"KAHH, KAHH, KAHH."

Baby then came toddling over.

"I'm not afraid of germs. If you don't play with me, I'll cry."

Baby was on the verge of bursting into tears.

"Don't cry, don't cry!"

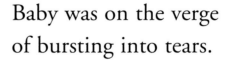

When suddenly…

"What a spoiled brat. Shut your big mouth."

Along with the voice, the paper doll on Chihiro's back fluttered down onto the floor. It suddenly became an old woman who looked just like Yubaba!

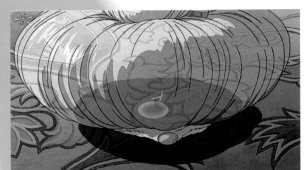

The old woman looked at Baby and said, "You're a bit of a porker, aren't you?"

HMMM. STILL SEE-THRU.

The old woman cast a spell on Baby and turned him into a little mouse.

"There, now, your body matches your brain."

Then

she proceeded to turn the Yu-Bird into a fly and the Kashira into Baby.

Chihiro was astonished. She asked her, "Who are you?"

"Zeniba, I'm Yubaba's twin sister. It was nice of you to lead me straight to this dragon's hiding place. Now hand him over to me."

"What do you want with Haku? He's

106

badly hurt."

"Too bad. He stole my solid-gold seal. It's magic and powerful, and I want it back."

"Haku wouldn't steal. He's a good person."

"Do you know why he became my sister's apprentice? To steal her magic secrets. And now he's stolen my magic too.

"Step aside, little girl. I'm going to take my seal back from him. There's a spell on the seal, and anyone who steals it will die."

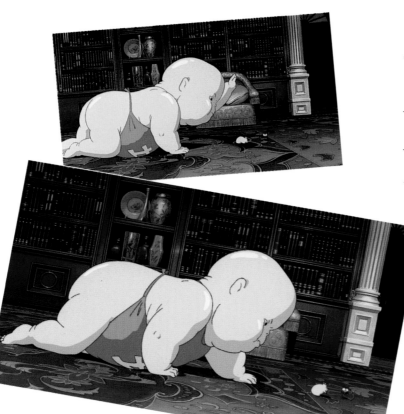

coming up here."

While Yubaba's sister was distracted by them, suddenly— "HAHH!"—the dragon lifted its head and cut the paper doll with his tail.

WHUMP, WHUMP! The floor was rumbling.

The Kashira that had been turned into Baby was trying to smash the little mouse and the fly.

"You idiots! What's your problem? Keep quiet! I don't want my sister

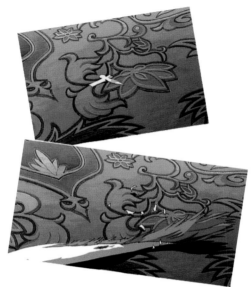

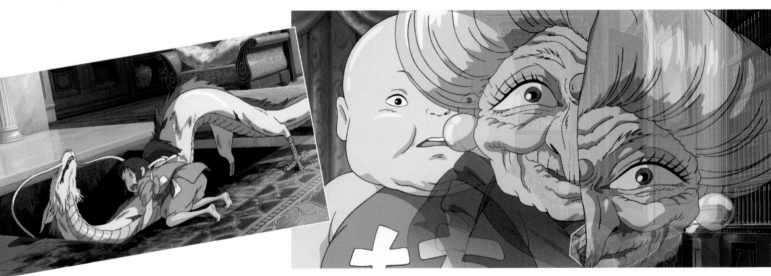

SLISH!

"Ow! A paper cut!"

Yubaba's sister was cut in half and disappeared. Then the dragon collapsed into

the hole.

"Haku, we're falling! Aieee!"

Chihiro held onto the dragon, and they fell into the dark hole.

The lifeless dragon continued falling through the darkness.

"Haku!"

Clutching onto his back, Chihiro screamed when she felt an odd sensation. "What is this…water?" Before she had any time to think, the dragon opened its eyes wide. There were dark shadows wriggling at the bottom of the hole, eagerly anticipating their fall.

It was a close call. With its last ounce of strength, the dragon

turned back and leaped into a hole in the wall.

There was an exit at the end of the hole.

No, it wasn't an exit. It was an exhaust fan! The dragon frantically flew into it.

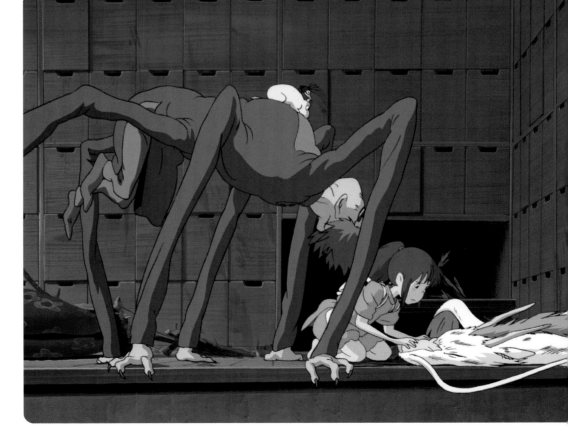

WHAT IS GOING ON HERE?

Kamaji
looked at the
dragon and said,
"This looks

KRRSH!
KRAK KRAK!
They burst
through the
exhaust fan
and fell into
Kamaji's boiler
room.

serious. It looks like he's bleeding from the inside."

MEDICINE FROM THE RIVER SPIRIT...

"From the inside?"

"I think so. Maybe he

swallowed something."

Chihiro took out her precious dumpling from her pocket.

"Haku, I got this gift from the River Spirit. Eat it, maybe it will help."

Chihiro bit it in half, pried open the dragon's mouth, and pushed it down its throat.

black slug and seal appeared.

"The gold seal!" Chihiro grabbed the seal and chased after the slug struggling to escape.

But it was jumping all over the place.

"HAHH! HAH, HAHH!" The dragon writhed in pain but then spat out something black and slimy.

"Get that black slug!" Kamaji yelled.

FSSH! As the slime melted away, a

OVER THERE! GET IT! GET IT!

Chihiro finally managed to crush the slug with her foot.

HURRY, BEFORE IT RUBS OFF ON YOU! PUT YOUR THUMBS AND FOREFINGERS TOGETHER.

!

EVIL BE GONE!

Showing the seal to Kamaji, Chihiro explained, "Haku stole this seal from Yubaba's sister."

"Zeniba's solid gold monogram seal? That's as powerful as it gets…"

The dragon turned back into Haku. Kamaji gave the frail boy an herbal soak. Then he put him on a futon bed.

"He just showed up out of nowhere. Just like you did. But he got mixed up with Yubaba and took a job as her apprentice. I warned him that it was too dangerous. 'Just quit and go back home,' I told him.

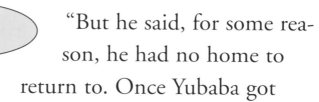

HAKU!

"But he said, for some reason, he had no home to return to. Once Yubaba got control over him, his face turned pale, and his eyes turned steely. He's never been the same."

HAKU! WAKE UP.

"Kamaji, what if I take the gold seal back to Zeniba? I could give back the seal and apologize to her for Haku. Can you tell me where Zeniba lives?"

"You'd go to Zeniba's? It might help, but she's one dangerous witch."

"Please? Haku helped me before. Now I want to help him."

"Hmm…"

That was when Lin showed up.

"I've looked everywhere for you! Yubaba is furious. The guy with all the gold turned out to be a monster called No Face. And she says you let him into the bath house."

"I did let him in."

"Are you serious?"

"Yeah, I thought he was a customer."

Kamaji then took out a packet of train tickets from one of his drawers and offered them to Chihiro.

"Now listen carefully. The train stop you want is called Swamp Bottom."

"'Swamp Bottom'?"

"That's where Zeniba lives. The sixth stop."

WHAT'S GOING ON?

SOMETHING YOU WOULDN'T RECOGNIZE. IT'S CALLED LOVE.

"Sixth stop."

Chihiro took the tickets and spoke to Haku, "Haku, I'll be back soon. Just hold on."

Before leaving though, Chihiro went to Yubaba's palace.

"Where is Sen? I want Sen!" No Face shouted in the parlor room.

Chihiro entered the parlor room and approached No Face alone.

No Face was now bloated from every-

thing he swallowed. He spoke in the assistant manager's voice, "Come closer, Sen. What would you like? Just name it."

"I would like to leave, Sir. You should go back to where you came from. Yubaba doesn't want you in the bath house any longer."

HE'S DESTROYING EVERYTHING! IT'S COSTING US A FORTUNE. SO SUCK UP TO HIM AND GET EVERY LAST SPECK OF GOLD!

No Face drooped his head, as if he were ashamed.

"Where is your home? Don't you have any friends or family?"

"No…no…I'm lonely…I'm lonely…"

No Face buried his face into this body, moaning, as he crawled up to Chihiro.

"I want Sen…I want Sen…"

"If you want to eat me, eat this first."

Chihiro tossed the rest of the dumpling into No Face's mouth.

"Ah…ah…oooh…"

No Face was writhing in pain and suddenly spit out something murky.

"AAARGH!"

No Face chased after her. Chihiro ran into the hall.

"HAAAK!"

"Sen…what did you do to me?" He was infuriated.

No one could stop No Face's rampage.

But Chihiro led No Face further and further outside.

The more he spat out, the weaker he became. He staggered as he chased after her.

Outside, Lin was waiting in the tub boat.

Seeing No Face still following her, Chihiro changed her clothes and yelled, "Hey, over here!"

Lin rowed the tub to the railway.

Chihiro stepped onto the railway and walked to the station.

Now that he had thrown up everything he had swallowed, No Face returned to his normal appearance and followed Chihiro like a shadow.

The train arrived
at the station.

"We'd like to go to
Swamp Bottom, please."

Chihiro gave her set of
train tickets. The
conductor counted the
passengers, Chihiro, the
mouse, and the fly...Then
he pointed behind her.

There was No Face
standing behind her.

"Oh, you want to come with us?" Chihiro asked.

No Face nodded several times. "Ah…ah…"

Chihiro said to the conductor, "He'd like to come too, please."

With everyone aboard, the train quietly began to depart.

The passengers got off the train one by one. By evening Chihiro and her friends were the only ones left.

Chihiro stared outside as the
train ran through the night.

Haku and Chihiro

Haku awoke in the dim boiler room. Kamaji was nodding off beside him. Haku got up and gently touched Kamaji's hand.

"Kamaji, wake up."
"Haku, you're all right?"

"I'm fine. Where is Sen? Did she go somewhere? Can you tell me what's going on?"

"You blacked out, remember?"

"Yeah, I remember being in darkness. Then I could hear Sen's voice calling out my name. I followed her voice, and the next thing I know, I was lying here, feeling better than ever."

"Pure love. It broke Zeniba's spell…"

SHE DID IT TO SAVE YOU…

Her bath house was nearly destroyed. Yubaba was furious.

"This gold doesn't even come close to covering the damage that stupid No Face caused. Sen didn't get nearly enough. She'll have to be punished…"

"Madame, you see, Sen was the one who saved us from No Face," the little green frog said.

Yubaba screamed back at him, "So what? This whole mess is her fault. And now she's run away from here. She's even abandoned

THOSE PIGS MUST BE READY TO EAT BY NOW. TURN THEM INTO BACON.

her own parents."

"Wait a minute."

It was Haku.

"You still haven't noticed something pre-cious to you has been replaced."

Haku stared into Yubaba's face.

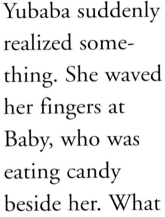

Yubaba suddenly realized some-thing. She waved her fingers at Baby, who was eating candy beside her. What a surprise! Baby turned back into the Kashira, and the gold turned into dirt.

AUGGHH!!

Yubaba's real Baby was nowhere to be seen!

"You…!"

Yubaba's was enraged. Her hair stood on end as she blew fire out at Haku.

With raging flames blowing in his face, Haku calmly replied, "He's with your sister."

"Zeniba?"

"I want you to return Sen and her mother and father back to the human world."

"Fine. But on one condition. If she fails she's mine."

It was completely dark by the time they reached Swamp Bottom station.

As Chihiro and her friends walked down the path from the station, something bright skipped towards them.

It was a lantern.

The lantern lit up the dark

path, guiding them to Zeniba's house.

They nervously stood in front of the house when the door swung open on its own.

They heard the voice of Zeniba say, "Come in."

Chihiro took a deep breath and stepped into the house.

"So you all made it." Zeniba offered them a warm welcome.

In return Chihiro offered the seal to Zeniba. "Excuse me, ma'am. Haku stole this from you. I came to give it back."

"I see. Do you have any idea what this is?"

Hearing how Chihiro had crushed the slug with the seal, Zeniba burst into laughter.

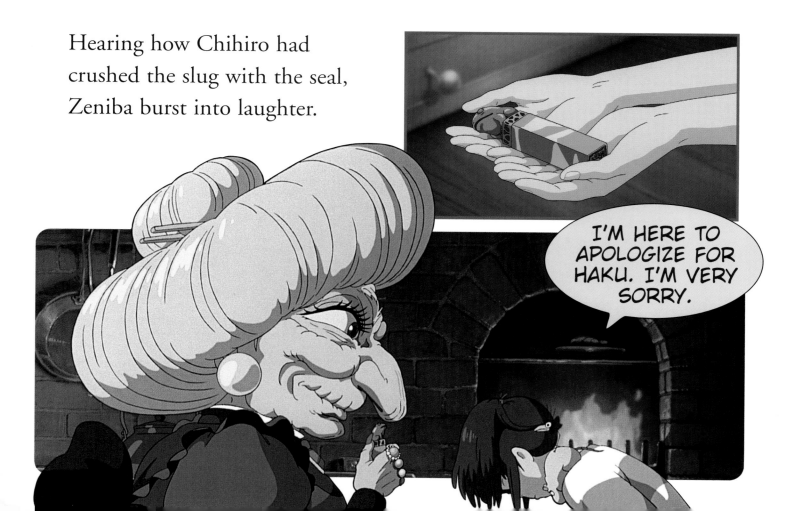

"HA HA HA HA. That wasn't my slug. My sister put that slug in Haku so she could control him.

"What happened to my spell? Only love can break it...Come now."

Zeniba offered chairs to Chihiro and No Face. She then told the mouse and the fly, "The spell on you two wore off long ago. Change back, if you want."

The mouse and the fly shook their heads. They liked the way they were.

As they sat down for tea, Chihiro told Zeniba how she ended up here.

Zeniba said, "I don't get along with my sister. She's so obnoxious. We're identical twins, yet exact opposites.

I'm sorry she turned your parents into pigs, but there's nothing I can do. It's just the way things are."

"You'll have to help your parents and Haku on your own. Use what you

remember about them."

"What? Can't you please give me more of a hint than that?

"It seems like I met Haku before, but it was a long time ago."

"That's a good start. Once you've met someone, you never really forget them. It just takes awhile for your memories to return. While you're thinking, the boys and I are going to make you something."

...

COME ON, KEEP AT IT.

urgent look and said, "Granny, I can't remember anything at all. Haku could be dead already, and I'm just sitting around here. My mom and dad could have been eaten for dinner."

No Face and the others helped Zeniba.

Chihiro gave Zeniba an

Zeniba then gave Chihiro the shining new band they just finished making.

"Use it to tie back your hair."

Zeniba looked into Chihiro's eyes and said, "It'll protect

you. It's made from the thread your friends wove together."

"Thank you." Chihiro said and proceeded to tie her hair with it.

The wind began to blow, rattling the windows.

"What good timing. We've got another guest. Will you let him in?" Zeniba said.

IT'S... BEAUTIFUL.

Chihiro opened the door. There was the white dragon. The dragon shook its green mane and whiskers in the air.

It was Haku! He had come to take Chihiro back.

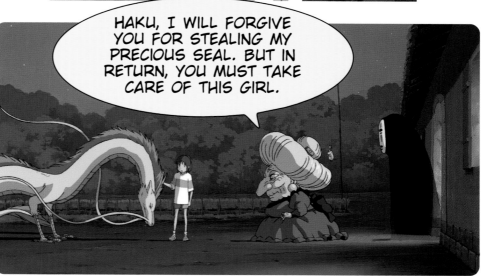

COME BACK SOON.

FP

NO FACE, WHY DON'T YOU STAY WITH ME, I COULD USE A GOOD HELPER.

AH... AH...

Haku took Chihiro and her friends and soared up into the sky. Zeniba's house became tinier and tinier as they climbed upwards.

GRANNY! THANK YOU SO MUCH. I'LL MISS YOU.

DON'T WORRY, YOU'LL BE ALL RIGHT, SEN.

I WANT YOU TO KNOW MY REAL NAME. IT'S CHIHIRO.

CHIHIRO... WHAT A PRETTY NAME. YOU TAKE GOOD CARE OF IT.

I WILL.

Haku soared gracefully through the beautiful moonlit sky.

Suddenly, Chihiro felt that familiar sensation again. This time she knew what it was.

A small child's
shoe…Then water
flowing against her
face…

"Haku, listen. I just remembered something from a long time ago. I think it may help you. Once when I was little, I dropped my shoe into a river. When I tried to get it, I fell in. I thought I'd drown, but the water carried me to shore. It finally came back to me…

"That river's

name was…the Kohaku River…

"I think that was you, and your real name is Kohaku River."

And that was when…

FSHAAA! Haku's scales scattered against the moonlit sky.

"You did it, Chihiro! I remember I was the spirit of the Kohaku River."

"A river spirit?"

"My name is the Kohaku River."

"They filled in that river. It's all apartments."

"That must be why I can't find my way home, Chihiro. I remember you falling into my river, and I remember your little pink shoe. So you

They held
each other's
hands, fly-
ing towards
the rising
sun.

were
the
one
who
carried me back into
the shallow water. You
saved me…I knew you
were good."

Dawn was breaking.

Everyone at the bath house was waiting anxiously for Chihiro and her

HEY! THERE THEY ARE!

MY BABY!

ARE YOU TRAUMATIZED?

friends' return.

Haku said, "Don't forget your promise. You must return Chihiro and her parents to the human world."

"Not so fast, Haku. I get to give Sen one final test."

With Chihiro's contract in her hand, Yubaba presented twelve pigs.

"See if you can tell which of these pigs are your mother and father."

"You get one try. If you get it right, you can all go home."

Everyone watched anxiously. Chihiro examined the pigs in front of her.

Chihiro said to Yubaba, "There must be a mistake. None of these pigs are my mom or dad."

"None of them? Is that really your answer?"

"Uhhh-humm."

Poof! The contract turned into smoke.

You got it!

"Way to go!"

"Hooray!"

Everyone shouted for joy.

GOOD BYE!

LET'S GO!

Haku led Chihiro back through the town.

WHERE ARE MY MOM AND DAD?

WHEN YOU PASSED THE TEST THEY WOKE UP ON THE HUMAN SIDE OF THE RIVER.

They stopped at the stone steps.

The water had vanished completely. It was now the wide open field she had seen before.

"I can't go any farther," Haku said.

THERE'S NO WATER HERE!

"Just go back the way you came, you'll be fine. But you have to promise not to look back—not until you've passed through the tunnel."

"What about you? What will you do?"

"Don't worry, I'll go back and have a talk with Yubaba. I'll tell her I'm going to quit being her apprentice. I'm fine. I got my name back."

"Will we meet again sometime?"

"I'm sure we will."

"Promise?"

"Promise. Now go. And don't look back."

Chihiro ran down the field alone.

"Chihiro! Where've you been? Hurry up!" It was her mother. Her father and mother were waiting by the tunnel. They were back. As if nothing had happened…

What then was that strange experience?

YOU SHOULDN'T RUN OFF LIKE THAT, HONEY.

ARE YOU GUYS SURE YOU'RE ALL RIGHT?

…

Chihiro did her best not to look back. Then she followed after her parents and entered the tunnel. She could only hear the sound of their footsteps echo in the tunnel.

EVERYBODY WATCH YOUR STEP.

CHIHIRO, DON'T CLING LIKE THAT. YOU'LL MAKE ME TRIP.

WE MADE IT.

HEY, WHAT HAPPENED?

WHAT IS IT?

LOOK AT THAT.

IT'S ALL DUSTY INSIDE, TOO.

IS THIS SOMEONE'S IDEA OF A JOKE?

...

COME ON, CHIHIRO.

LET'S GET TO OUR NEW HOME.

Somewhere, a voice calls, in the depths of my heart
May I always be dreaming, the dreams that move my heart

So many tears, of sadness, uncountable through and through
I know on the other side, of them, I'll find you

Every time we fall down to the ground, we look up to the blue sky above
We wake to its blueness, as for the first time
Though the road is long and lonely and the end far away, out of sight
I can with these two arms, embrace the light

As I bid farewell, my heart stops, in tenderness I feel
My silent empty body begins to listen to what is real

The wonder of living, the wonder of dying
The wind, town and flowers, we all dance one unity

Somewhere, a voice calls in the depths of my heart
Keep dreaming your dreams, don't ever let them part

Why speak of all your sadness or of life's painful woes
Instead let the same lips sing a gentle song for you

The whispering voice, we never want to forget, in each passing memory
Always there to guide you
When a mirror has been broken, shattered pieces scattered on the ground
Glimpses of new life, reflected all around

Window of beginning, stillness, new light of the dawn
Let my silent empty body be filled and reborn

No need to search outside, nor sail across the sea
Cause here shining inside me, it's right here inside me
I've found a brightness, it's always with me

WALT DISNEY STUDIOS PRESENTS
A STUDIO GHIBLI FILM

MIYAZAKI'S
SPIRITED AWAY
Picture Book

SPIRITED AWAY PICTURE BOOK

ORIGINAL STORY AND SCREENPLAY
WRITTEN AND DIRECTED BY HAYAO MIYAZAKI

English Adaptation/Yuji Oniki
Design and Layout/Izumi Evers

Sen to Chihiro no Kamikakushi (Spirited Away) © 2001 Studio Ghigli - NDDTM
All rights reserved. First published by Tokuma Shoten Co., Ltd. in Japan.

Printed in China

Published by VIZ Media, LLC
P.O. Box 77010, San Francisco, CA 94107

First printing, October 2002
Sixth printing, August 2018

Visit **www.viz.com**